Ballerina Bright

FINDS HER VOICE

written by: ELLEN REED

SHAYNA YACYSHYN

pictures by:

A special thank you to #TeamBallerinaBright. Each of you helped bring this dream and book to fruition.

To my illustrator Shayna Yacyshyn of quirky burp illustrations: Thank you for your love, support, and contribution towards the publication of Ballerina Bright Finds Her Voice.

To my life coach Amie Crites : Thank you for supporting and guiding me through the process of writing and publishing my first children's book.

To my sister and guardian angel Cari Reed who watches over me daily: I love you.

Ballerina Bright was daydreaming in her room. She was dancing on a bright tie-dyed stage. The stage was covered with every color of the rainbow.

She was daydreaming that she had helped others through her dancing. That made her feel good. She loved dancing and loved seeing others happy.

Ballerina Bright wasn't your typical ballerina. She loved wearing leggings and an oversized tie-dyed shirt. Sometimes she would wear shoes and sometimes not - who really needed them? When she wasn't daydreaming, she was busy spreading joy.

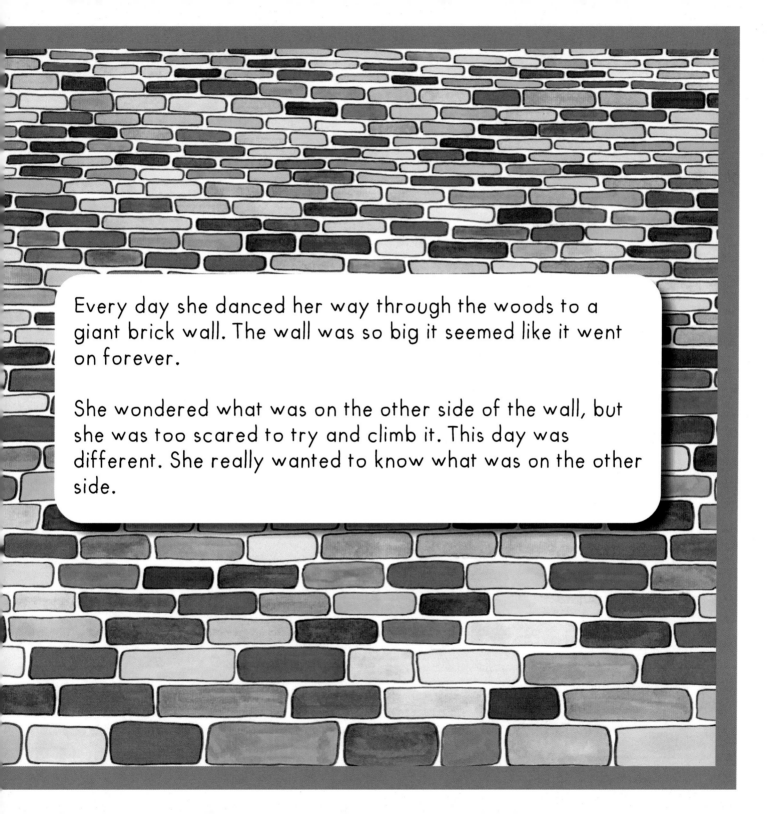

Every day she danced her way through the woods to a giant brick wall. The wall was so big it seemed like it went on forever.

She wondered what was on the other side of the wall, but she was too scared to try and climb it. This day was different. She really wanted to know what was on the other side.

As she stepped closer to get a better look at the wall, she realized there was something written on one of the bricks. All she could make out were the words,

I AM CONFIDENT

and she thought that was strange.

A woman was sitting nearby. Ballerina Bright danced over to her to ask her how to get over the wall. The woman looked at her and said...

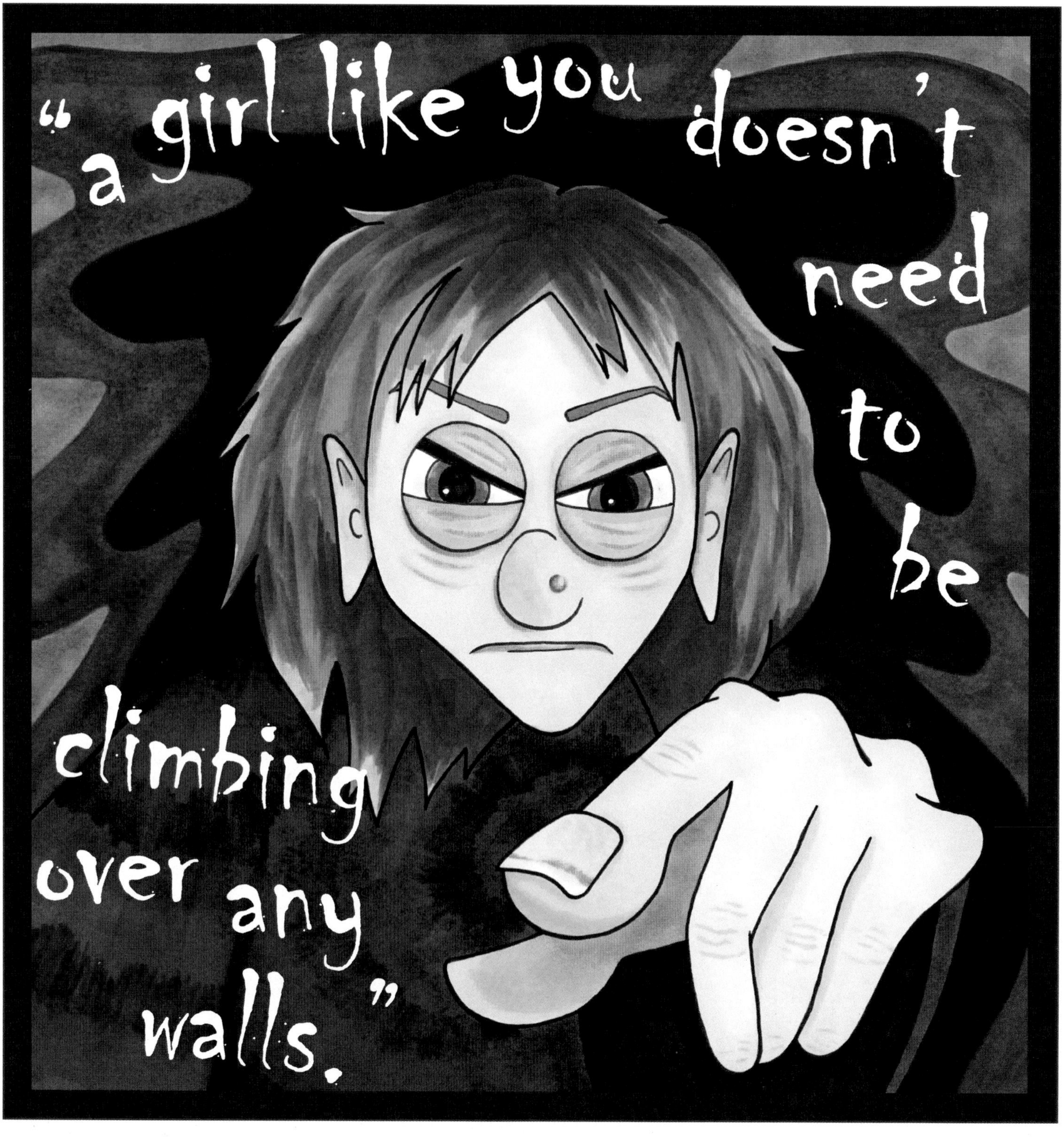
"a girl like you doesn't need to be climbing over any walls."

Ballerina Bright curled up in her bed. She tossed and turned. Ballerina Bright dreamt about the woman who dismissed her earlier in the day. She woke up startled.

She decided right then "**I AM CONFIDENT**" and I will get over that wall. She pictured herself getting over the wall and fell peacefully back to sleep snuggling her cat.

The next day Ballerina Bright made her way down to the brick wall. She found the woman from the day before standing there. The woman began to yell...

"You will never figure this out never go beyond

and you will that wall. "

Ballerina Bright started to believe the woman and began to walk away crying when suddenly she remembered the writing on the wall.

She stopped and turned around staring up at the words "I AM CONFIDENT."

She began repeating it aloud. "I AM CONFIDENT. I AM CONFIDENT."

Something began to happen. The brick began to shake.
She said it again only this time louder. **"I AM CONFIDENT!"** The
brick came crumbling down. How interesting she thought.

Ballerina Bright tried to jump up to see what was on the other side of the wall,

meow

but she wasn't tall enough.

She tried to climb the wall and that didn't work either.

Suddenly, she heard the woman yelling about how she wasn't big enough or tall enough to get over the wall.

The woman looked a bit shocked but still insisted on giving Ballerina Bright a hard time. The woman laughed and said, "Keep trying, you're only going to fail."

Ballerina Bright was determined to prove to herself she could get over the wall. She walked a little further down and found more words written on the wall. This time it was closer to the ground. She started to read it aloud. **"I AM STRONG**," she said. The woman muttered, "Not strong enough to get over the wall."

Ballerina Bright dug her feet deep into the ground and took the biggest breath possible and began to scream,

I AM STRONG, I AM ENOUGH, I AM CONFIDENT!

The whole wall came tumbling down!

Ballerina Bright did it! She believed in herself more than the woman who doubted her. She stayed consistent and committed.

Now, she was able to see what was on the other side of the wall. She was so excited!

To her surprise she saw a giant stage! It was bright and tie-dyed with every color of the rainbow just like the one she had been daydreaming about! As she started to dance towards the stage, she heard the woman say something else.

"Good job kid. I didn't think you could get past the wall but you did. I'm sorry I was so hard on you."

Ballerina Bright's eyes lit up. She looked at the woman and said, "Thank you for apologizing. Sometimes we have to try even when others don't believe in us."

The woman smiled as Ballerina Bright reached her hand out as an invitation to join her on stage. Ballerina Bright's dream came true!

The End

Ballerina Bright's adventure continues.
Where will she end up next?

Ellen Reed, Author

Facebook.com/
StoryTellingWithEllen

StoryTellingWithEllen@
gmail.com

Ellen Reed received her Early Education and Care Certificate in 2006, and is the owner and operator of Storytelling with Ellen. Ellen has worked with children in daycare settings since 2002. Faced with challenges since the day she was born, Ellen wrote her first children's book "Ballerina Bright Finds Her Voice" as a way to encourage children to never give up when facing challenges. In 2021, she began offering educational coaching virtually for children ages 5-8. When Ellen isn't writing, reading or coaching, she enjoys diamond painting and hanging out with Talia, her cat.

Shayna Yacyshyn, Illustrator

 @quirky_burp

 quirkyburp.com

Shayna Yacyshyn received her BA in Illustration in 2018 from Framingham State University, and is the owner and artist behind the stationary and custom art business, quirky burp illustrations. Shayna is making her debut as a children's book illustrator with "Ballerina Bright Finds Her Voice" and could not have found a more compassionate and inspiring author to work with. Shayna resides in Massachusetts where she enjoys exploring different cuisines and roller skating.

Cosmic Creations Publishing Inc.
3822 S. Westmont Ave.
Bloomington, IN 47403 US
www.CosmicCreationsPublishing.com

For inquiries about volume orders, please contact:
info@cosmiccreationspublishing.com

Published in the United States by Cosmic Creations Publishing Inc.
Distributed by Cosmic Creations Publishing Inc.
Author: Ellen Reed
Cover Design, Interior Design and Illustrations: Shayna Yacyshyn of quirky burp
Editors: Amie Crites, Debbie Goodman and Amber Goodman of Cosmic Creations Publishing

Made in the USA
Columbia, SC
21 November 2022